RUSH JOB
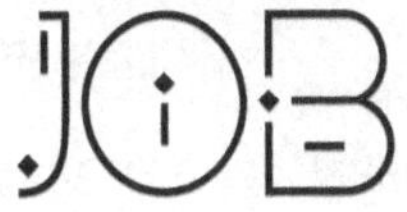

AMY LAURENS

AUSTRALIA

Print ISBN: 978-1-922434-08-1
eBook ISBN: 9781393872412

www.inkprintpress.com

National Library of Australia Cataloguing-in-Publication Data
Laurens, Amy 1985—
Rush Job
76 p.   cm.
ISBN: 978-1-922434-08-1
Inkprint Press, Canberra, Australia
1. Fiction—Science Fiction—Crime & Mystery 2. Fiction—
Science Fiction—Action & Adventure

Summary: A visit to neutral space station Aphelion becomes a rush heist job for the Inter-Galactic Police when Jamie receives news of Clan Witches on board.

First Edition: February 2021

Cover design © Inkprint Press.

Rush Job

AMY LAURENS

OTHER WORKS

SANCTUARY SERIES

Where Shadows Rise
Through Roads Between
When Worlds Collide
The Complete Sanctuary Series

KADITEOS SERIES

How Not To Acquire A Castle

STORM FOXES SERIES

A Fox Of Storms And Starlight

SHORTER WORKS

Darkness and Good
Dreaming Of Forests
It All Changes Now
Of Sea Foam and Blood
Rush Job
Trust Issues

NON-FICTION

How To Create Cultures
How To Create Life
How To Map
How To Theme
How To Write Dogs
The 32 Worst Mistakes People Make About Dogs

Find other works by the author at
www.amylaurens.com/books/

RUSH JOB

On the polished-white perspex desk by the holovid, the tiny grey printer chattered. The little stream of paper it was sending out into the dim room was no more than a handsbreadth across, and in the blue light of the sleeping screens the paper glowed cerulean.

Jamie Evans leaned back in her moulded desk chair, waiting for the printer to finish. The warm scent of the ink clouded around her and she drummed her fingers on the desk, impatient to see what the orders would bring.

The printer chattered on.

Jamie glanced up at the holoscreens that towered from her desk surface right up to the roof, wrapping around her in a glowing blue semi-circle in the small, dark control room of her shuttle. The screens continued their sleep though, devoid of any new information.

Out of habit, she checked the navsystem: all clear, everything still on track, the shuttle scheduled to arrive at the space station Aphelion in a little over two hours.

Jamie drummed her fingers again as the printer continued its chatter. Damn thing never was fast enough.

She stretched languidly in her chair, briefly considered that she should maybe grab something to eat as her stomach rumbled, then decided against it as memories of her last visit to Aphelion surfaced.

Aphelion's marketplace was famous throughout the entirety of clean space, with every kind of food—and every kind of human—in attendance. Along with a fair few other things, including everything you usually had to travel to Clan Space for.

Jamie's lips quirked. Last time, she'd come away with a lifelong love for pecan cheesecake, a pocket scanner that should have taken two months and four thousand bucks to source if she'd done it legal, and a voucher for a dinner at Maxador, rumoured to be the best restaurant in not just this quadrant, but the entire galaxy.

Even the Witch Clans, it was rumoured, couldn't do better than Maxador.

Jamie stretched again and sighed. It was fifty-fifty whether she'd have time to cash in on that dinner on this trip. It all hinged on that strip of paper now trailing over the edge of the desk from the little printer.

The printer beeped, green light flashing.

Ha. At last. You'd have thought, Jamie mused, that in this day and age someone could invent a cryptron printer that was faster.

Jamie leaned forward, tore off the strip of paper, and turned it over. Arcane-looking symbols covered it in neat, diagonal lines. She squinted. She'd been receiving her orders in cryptron for eight years now, and despite the fact that it was designed to be an infallibly uncrackable cipher unless you had one of the patented and heavily legislated readers, some days she felt she was getting the hang of it. That series of markings there, for example.

Her heart sped up.

Unless she was highly mistaken, that little cluster meant a job with a tight deadline.

Jamie spun the chair around, tapped the control panel on the other side of desk to wake the reader, and fed the long slip of paper into the slot in the interface.

A portion of the screen at the lower left lit up, white code streaming past on a blue background, designed not to provide any actually information, but merely to make it look like the machine was doing something useful. Jamie knew. She'd copied all the code down in her first year and broken it. *Lorem ipsum dolor sit amet...* It was all nonsense.

She drummed her fingers again.

The scent of warm spices curled around her.

"Hello-Alex?"

"Hello, Jamie," the ship's AI responded in soothing, neutral tones.

"Why can I smell yellow curry?"

"It is thirteen hundred ship time. It is time for you to ingest sustenance."

Jamie sighed. Forgetting to reschedule the automatic meal system wasn't the worst thing in the world. And if this really was a rush job the cryptron reader was presently decoding, maybe it was better to eat here first.

The lower-left screen flashed green. The torrent of nonsense code gave way to a series of runic markings on screen—Cyrillic, a millennia-dead language revived explicitly for this purpose when cryptron was invented, because there was no point having an unhackable cipher if you also had a machine that could simply translate it into Standard. There were legislations around ownership of the readers, sure, but it would be stupid to assume that in the whole history and use of cryptron, no one would ever illegally procure a reader. Or crack the code.

Cyrillic, though, Jamie could read no problem. The gist of the situation was this: in about nine hours, a deal was going down somewhere in the marketplace on Aphelion, probably Sector Q. Maybe P.

A rare—and priceless—stolen item was being traded. The government needed the item back. Jamie was to retrieve it.

There were more details, of course: general description of the item, possible parties involved in the trade, blah blah, etc etc.

Jamie stopped. Squinted at the page. Reread it, just to make sure her Cyrillic wasn't off.

The item she was supposed to collect was a spherical, gelatinous object about two feet in diameter. It was listed as organic, virtually indestructible, and preferring vacuum for long-term transport.

Jamie squinted again. "Hello-Alex?"

"Hello, Jamie."

"Read this." She motioned at one of Alex's many camera eyes set around the room, their lenses no more than an inch across. "What does this sound like to you?"

"Item category best fits that of a space egg."

Jamie's stomach flipped. "Yeah. That's what I thought."

There were still a few surviving species that did space eggs of that size, shape and colour. It was plausible—and probable—that this was no particularly big deal, just a species the IGP wanted their hands on. This was not the 2600s. Surrofish had died out over 400 years ago.

It was not a surrofish egg, because that would be stupid—and disastrous.

Jamie chewed at the inside of her lip.

A century or two after humans colonised space, they'd realised they weren't alone. There were other creatures out there in the black, not sentient, but smart in their own ways.

These creatures lived in the vacuum, a complex, delicate ecosystem built on living particles similar to tardigrades—single-celled and nearly indestructible.

They formed the bottom of a food web as complex and varied as the one built on plankton. And for the most part, these creatures of vacuum were about as dangerous to humans as ocean creatures were—keep out of their way and they'd keep out of yours.

Then the Witches, a group of superpowered and highly xenophobic humans, had found the surrofish, whose eggs could support the bacteria the Witches used to maintain their super-powers—and which sent normal humans fatally insane.

A surrofish egg could survive vacuum indefinitely, and at only two-feet in width, they were nigh undetectable to radars attuned to larger threats.

And loaded up with Witch bacteria, they could seed the terraforming of an entire planet, letting loose a pathogen that would destroy any clean humans on the planet within months.

It was the galactic equivalent to all-out nuclear warfare, and it only ended when the IGP—Inter-Galactic Police, the enforcement arm of the united government of clean-human space—had engineered a gene drive that sent the surrofish extinct.

A tiny, possibly concerned beep. "Is anything wrong?" Alex enquired.

Jamie shook her head, hauling herself out of the dark well of her thoughts. "No. I'm being absurd. Alarmist. Like the plague, you know? Mention a rat infestation and people's minds *still* go back to the great Earth plagues of the 1400s."

"I am aware of this connection."

Jamie sighed. So she had to retrieve a space egg. There were plenty of species that laid space eggs. Totally no big deal. And if she worked fast enough, her IGP orders wouldn't interfere with her plans to see Nathaniel. Again.

She rechecked the navsys. One hour and forty-six minutes to prep. Plenty of time.

Right after she ate that curry.

The spices of the curry lingering in the corners of her mouth, Jamie entered the dark toy room. "Hello-Alex, lights please."

Lights came up, illuminating the square room with its silver walls and black floor. About four paces square, the walls were lined top to bottom in assorted weapons: projectiles, both old-style and new; blunt-force weapons; blades of every size and shape; chains, defensive shields, more.

In the middle, a square table lit up also, inset lights illuminating the clear perspex boxes forming the perfect square of its surface, housing more than a hundred useful gadgets.

Jamie headed for the table, the scent of wintergreen cleaner and astringent solvent enveloping her. The weapons on the walls were useless for this job; Aphelion had a strict no-violence policy, and tried to enforce a weapons-free environment as best as it could. The AI, Satomi, reputedly knew every extant projectile on sight—and her information network was fast, learning of new tools on the market often within hours of their creation.

So... Nothing on the walls would help. Jamie surveyed the table, tapping a fingernail on the clear surface.

She sighed. It was a straight in-and-out. Find rendezvous, sabotage rendezvous, steal item, get out. Possibly she could even reclaim the item before or after the designated handover, too, which would be far less flashy and much quieter.

But either way, it wasn't a complicated job.

She tapped the perspex lids over a few of the boxes. A couple of buzzballs to protect her from unwanted physical contact (of all varieties) and to act as an emergency shield for the target. A pattern scanner, definitely—they were invaluable in detecting places that people wanted other people kept away from. A general goodies bag of bugs and minicams and sundry other surveillance essentials. A counterblock beam so she could disrupt *other* people's surveillance. One or two other little things, then she clicked all the perspex boxes closed again.

That'd do.

Jamie slotted the various devices into her work belt, a three-inch contoured black band that sat perfectly over her favourite midnight blue jodhpurs and was mostly hidden by her similarly-coloured work blazer, the one that looked formal and profesh but was stretchy as putty and gave her plenty of movement range. Then she flicked a couple of switches on the belt, double checking the counter-surv shields.

"Hello-Alex, confirm you can access belt for software upgrades."

"Hello, Jamie. Confirmed: your belt is 99.99% functional."

She arched an eyebrow. "Point nine-nine?"

"There is a thread loose in the fabric below the shield input port."

Jamie sniffed, but still pulled the thread free. "Better?"

"No. Now there is a thread missing from the weft."

Jamie rolled her eyes. "Thanks, Alex."

"You are welcome."

Geared and ready to work, Jamie opened two last boxes. From one, she pulled out a packet of fresh fingerprints. She ripped the plastic open, squeezed a tiny dab of fumey glue onto each, and adhered them to her fingertips.

From the other box came a set of bright blue contact lenses. Jamie pivoted to the wall and slid them in, blinking in irritation as the plastic slips settled in over her eyes. "I hate these things," she muttered. "Feels like I'm wearing plastic wrap over my eyeballs."

"You have noted this," Alex said in a voice that would have been dry if Alex had been capable of modulating their voice.

"Time check?" Jamie said, eyeing her reflection critically. She squinted her left eye and the contacts telescoped her vision in, providing her with a close up of the wall behind her. She squinted the right and the lenses zoomed back to regular vision.

"Fifty-seven minutes. Recommend engage docking sequence in eleven minutes."

"Copy that."

Jamie tugged the hairband from her dark hair. Eleven minutes. Just long enough to braid her hair out of the way, and she'd be good to go.

The sterile air of the station's customs hall wound around Jamie like it meant business and didn't care what hers was. On the pretence of smoothing down her navy blue blazer, Jamie ran her hands over and around her broad belt, checking her equipment was still in place after her walk through the decontamination zone. The taste of the antiseptics still lingered in the back of her throat, astringent and chemical.

Satisfied her tools had made it through unchanged, Jamie hitched the small backpack stuffed with a towel that she had only for pretenses—security tended to be suspicious of people arriving on station without luggage—and joined the long queue of people in a line that wound back and forth across the wide hall, following the trail delineated for them by retractable black guide ropes.

She eyed the customs stations ahead as the muted chatter of people applying for entry to the station echoed around the double-storey ceiling.

Nineteen stations, twelve currently operational. The line snaked from one side of the room to the other three and a half times. Maybe forty people for each length of the room. Two minutes per group, say an average of two people per group. With twelve operational stations, that was... just under twelve minutes.

Lips pursed, Jamie tapped her watch. 15:26 shuttle time, which was... She cycled through the available time zones on the watch. There. 17:40 local. Her lips pressed tighter. She'd told Nathaniel she'd be here at 17:45.

Jamie glanced up at the queue again as the line moved up.

At least five minutes until Nathaniel could run interference and pull her out of this. Eleven minutes to the head of the queue.

No worries.

She hefted the small backpack again and tucked her thumbs under the straps nonchalantly. The weight of the towel was negligible. Easy to ignore.

Much easier than ignoring her toolbelt with its goodies of questionable legality.

The queue shuffled forward, people murmuring and muttering. Despite the heavily filtered air, the smell of human sweat lingered.

17:43. Nathaniel should be just around the corner.

Despite herself, Jamie lifted her chin a little to peer beyond the customs stations. Brunettes, blonds, lots of black hair. Green and blue were in fashion right now too, it seemed, with some purple thrown in for good measure.

Nathaniel's distinctive fire-orange was, however, notably absent.

Jamie caught herself tapping her foot and stopped. It didn't matter; enough people in the queue were looking miserable and impatient that she'd blend right in as just one more weary traveller, ready for their journey to be over.

And Witches knew she'd had plenty of practice keeping her heart rate steady, lying to people's faces.

It wasn't that she was worried about getting *caught*, per se, trying to smuggle in a small host of items that Aphelion's AI Satomi would recognise at once as modified weapons. IGP would cut her loose if she did, though, and *pfft*, there went her steady pay cheque. She'd been on the other side of the spy game before, and she was here to assure anyone who wanted to listen that while crime could and occasionally did pay well, nothing beat the feeling of a regular salary turning up in your bank account without the nauseating accompaniment of wondering whether this was the time you'd screwed up and someone would trace you and lock you away.

17:46. Nathaniel was late.

Jamie sighed. The line was moving too fast for her liking—she was halfway through it now, a little over one and a half rows to go.

17:47.

They'd take her into custody, first things first. Satomi would likely interview her. Depending on how good her lying was, they might or might not call IGP after that.

IGP would send someone to investigate, just for the look of things, just so there was no way of tracing—Jamie glanced down at the e-pass on her watch—*Delilah Sampson* back to them.

And then they'd cut her loose, and she'd wind up in the prison system if she was lucky, and on a trade ship to Clan Space if not.

She squinted her left eye. The contact lenses that protected her original iris data from the ID scans and assisted her vision telescoped in. She searched the milling people beyond the customs stations, hoping that somewhere out there in the long hallway of humanity, she could spot Nathaniel.

17:49. Two and a half minutes before this mission, her career, and her autonomy were cut short.

It was no good. She'd have to back track, pretend she'd left something in decontam, see if they'd let her back through. It'd raise hella suspicion on her and there'd be no way she'd be able to come back through this port. She'd have to get back to Alex, kit out with new fingers, new irises, and try Aphelion's Delta Port halfway around the other side of the station.

She turned the final switchback in the line.

Her watch bipped.

She opened the message in the periphery of her contact lenses with a blink.

:Incoming:

Jamie glanced up in time to see Nathaniel flashing his pass at the nearest customs station with a smile dazzling enough to match his hot-orange hair.

He strode toward her, bouncing on his toes. "Hey," he said as he unclipped the guide rope next to her, ushered her through, and clipped it shut behind her.

"Hey yourself," Jamie said, gaze darting around to room to check who was watching. A few casual observers watched her go with envy, but for the most part, everyone was too concerned with their own needs and companions to pay her much mind. "What took you so long?"

Nathaniel gave her a sideways glance as he flashed his pass again at the bored, dark-skinned woman staffing the nearest customs station. "She's with me," he told the woman. "Priority clearance."

The woman nodded idly and thumbed the button to open the gate. "Pass," she said, tapping a small screen to Jamie's right.

Jamie held her watch up against it as she walked through the gate. The green beep that usually triggered the gates to open was a mere formality; the woman wasn't even looking any more.

Jamie breathed deeply as they walked away from the gate. "Next time," she said, "I'd appreciate you not cutting it so fine."

Nathaniel grinned. "I dunno, I would've liked to see you kick their butts."

Jamie arched an eyebrow as a cloud of perfume from one of the stores in the welcome hall surrounded them. "No butt-kicking would have been involved. I don't want to get spaced, thanks."

Blergh. Now her mouth tasted like over-priced perfume.

"Yeah, yeah." Nathaniel rolled his eyes exaggeratedly as they joined the throng of people milling up and down the mall strip. "I know. So what are you in town for this time? I suppose it's too much to ask that you came to see me?" He smiled about it good-naturedly, but Jamie knew the question was still pointed enough.

"Can we talk off the record somewhere?" Not only were there too many live ears around, visitors and station natives and shop workers alike, Satomi surveilled the welcome mall meticulously—just like nearly every other area of her domain.

Nathaniel's lips quirked. "Straight to that, hey."

Jamie eyed him sideways as she dodged a pram with a screaming toddler. "Does it help if I say I was actually planning to come spend time with you this time?"

He side-eyed her back. "Only if I think you're telling the truth."

Jamie sniffed.

They slowed outside a door set back several paces in an alcove between two shops. Stark, blocky letters on it proclaimed 'SECURITY: AUTHORISED PERSONNEL ONLY'.

Nathaniel swiped his pass and ushered her in.

The beige hall in front of them was longer than someone would have expected, seeing it the first time. This was not, however, the first time Jamie had seen it, or others like it, on this station. It *was* the first time it had ever smelled slightly damp and mouldy, though.

Jamie wrinkled her nose. "Cleaning staff on strike?"

Nathaniel snorted in response.

Halfway down, they stopped at another door on the right. Nathaniel swiped again, pressed his palm against the print scanner, stared into the retina scan, and finally extracted a real-life old-fashioned silver key from his pocket. It was tied on a loop, presumably so he couldn't lose it, and he had to do an awkward sort of jiggle to get it to reach the lock. He managed, though, and once again held the door for Jamie to enter.

It closed behind them with a heavy thunk, sealing out sound and most of the light. The little chamber they'd entered—about two point five metres square—was lit only by a single, dim bulb in the roof, its fluorescent light dripping down through the room in fits and starts.

Jamie inhaled deeply. "Air tight?" she said. The place had the familiar, slightly-dry feel of a contained air system.

Nathaniel nodded. He finished tucking the key away and leaned against one of the beige walls, arms folded. "Were you really coming to see me?"

Jamie shrugged. "Check my transmission records, if you like. I only got the call a couple of hours ago."

He stared at her for a long moment, dark brown eyes burrowing into her. Then he nodded. "Okay, I'll buy it. Thanks. What do you need?"

Quickly, she tapped her watch, sending a series of images to his similar—though slightly less *embellished*—one: a collection of photos of the man IGP MishCon had informed her was the likely candidate for the drop today.

Nathaniel made some adjustments, tilted his watch, and projected the first image onto the wall for easy viewing.

The little intake of breath as the image of the dark-haired, light-skinned, green-eyed man appeared on the wall was not a good sign.

"What is it?" Jamie asked.

"I'm guessing you want to know if he's on station," Nathaniel said, staring at the image.

Jamie nodded. "Yeah."

Nathaniel switched the projection off and turned to her. "He's on station alright. Arrived a little over twenty-four hours ago."

Jamie's spine itched. "So what's the problem?"

Suspect was on station, timing was right... The job had a tight deadline, sure, but it still seemed like a quick in-and-out.

Nathaniel stared at her, something hollow—fearful?—in his expression.

"What?" Jamie prompted, impatient.

"Witches," he said flatly. "Adan is on board alright. And he arrived with two Witches."

Adrenalin shot through Jamie's gut. Witches. Suck. "Do you know what Clan they are?"

Nathaniel shook his head. "No idea. They've got some sort of scan-blocking tech on them, even Satomi can't a fix on their ID."

Jamie pursed her lips firmly and nodded. "It's fine," she said, plans already spinning through her mind. "I'll handle it."

Satomi might not have been able to get a fix on the Witches' ID, but the station AI had been designed to run the tasks needed to support a human population of nearly a million on a space station all at once. She was hyper-intelligent, but she was a generalist.

Alex, on the other hand, had been designed with one thing in mind: spy work. Nat had extracted the best pictures he could find of the Witches from Satomi's database and forwarded them to Jamie, who'd forwarded them to Alex to work on.

And while Alex worked on cracking the Witches' ID, Jamie did the groundwork. Now, deep in Sector Q of the Aphelion marketplace, surrounded by living plants from every planet and station imaginable, Jamie sighed a sigh that tasted of sap and potting mix.

Witches. Suck. That was all she needed.

She could still hope it was coincidence. Hope they were here for something else.

But Adan had arrived with them, so hoping right now was the even-stupider equivalent of going for a space walk without your helmet on.

Suck.

Jamie ambled through the stalls, completely nonchalant to an observing eye, letting the pattern scanner she'd packed do its thing while she—for all intents and purposes—browsed. The false sky twenty, thirty storeys above was clear and blue and deep, spanning the vast field of the marketplace just like a real sky. She knew a few people—like Nat—who'd never seen a real sky, but she'd seen a few now in her lifetime and she was here to reassure anyone who cared that Aphelion's tech-sky was a masterpiece.

Down here, in the thick of Sector Q, stalls sprouted up like fungi along something that sort of approximated straight paths, but which curved gently, meandering a little more than in the other sectors. The floor here was gravel, matching the plant theme of the sector, and the multi-storey stalls were wooden, most with hanging gardens or ivy-covered awnings or vine-laden pergolas instead of marquees.

Some of the stalls were a rambling mess, selling anything and everything the proprietor found interesting. But most of them specialised, this one selling fruit trees, that one selling vegetables, another selling plants with medicinal uses—and others plants with 'medicinal' uses.

Jamie wandered through them all, deliberately walking close so the leaves trailed against her—huge, spiky rib-fans, flashing gold-and-silver Precious Apples, soft, frothy maiden's hair and furry little amzears.

All the while, the scanner bipped along, sweeping the area for bugs and other surveillance, tracking the irregular pattern of the stalls, monitoring the ebb and flow of the crowd, searching for anomalies.

It was behind a medicinal stall right by the outer wall of the marketplace—where vines twined and twisted up the wall that extended right up to the ceiling, some eighty, ninety metres straight up with nothing but synthstone and the windows of the apartments that filled the walls—that the scanner buzzed.

Jamie had lapped the sector twice—and something here, in this quiet corner where the buzz and drone of insects was as loud as the crowd's murmuring voices, had triggered the scanner's attention.

Almost absently, Jamie flicked a tiny on-off switch on her belt. Her skin tingled as the counter-surv activated. It wouldn't block her completely from bugs and microcams, but it would distort the data enough that whoever was watching wouldn't be able to get a lock on her ID.

The Witches were probably using something similar, and equally illegal on Aphelion.

Jamie's incoming messages pinged.

Visual message from Alex.

She relayed it to her contacts and scrolled down the message.

A photograph of a pale man with a narrow chin, sandy-brown hair, and the pinched, mean eyes of someone who picked fights for a living.

Suspect One: Positive ID.

Noma: Rob Chisholm.

Clan: Cerulean.

Blighted, acid-sucking contagion.

Clan Cerulean? That was just about as bad as things could be. The only thing worse would be…

Her chest constricted as the second photo appeared below the first set of data, a tall, regal, olive-skinned woman with dark hair and large eyes. She was dressed in the plain beige of a station worker, but there was no hiding—even in a photo-graph—the air of authority she wore over it.

Suspect Two: Positive ID.

Noma: Vivian Aaliyah.

Clan: Indigo.

Great. Just acid-sucking great. Two Witches on a station where they hadn't been seen in centuries, and she had to get an acid-sucking Cerulean *and* an Indigo: not just a Witch who could control minds, but a second one with precognitive powers.

What.

The.

Hell.

:Hey, Nat: she sent via the comms on her watch. :You know that mind-blocker you were prototyping last time I was here? How'd the testing go?:

:Acid-sucking,: he sent back almost immediately, the line of text popping up in Jamie's lower peripheral vision. :Clan Cerulean?:

:Yep. And an Indigo.:

:SUCK. NOT GOOD, JAMIE. Sure you don't wanna just reconvene and try again later?:

:Funny,: Jamie sent. :Just send me the codes for the mind-blocker.:

:babe u better come back alive,: Nat replied. :Ain't got leave to be attending funerals.:

:Haven't died yet. Codes???:

There was a brief moment of silence, and Jamie scanned the crowd around her. Nothing out of the ordinary; shoppers of all ages and body types and skin colours and hairstyles and dress milling slowly as they shopped and gathered and browsed.

Her watch pinged.

She pulled the code up on her lenses and skimmed through it. :You sure this'll work?:

:Best I've got.:

Jamie sighed. Well, she had a few hours yet. Maybe she could rig something so she wouldn't have to get near the Cerulean.

The precog would still be a problem, though. Depending on how good they were, they'd be able to see anything she planned.

With a dismissive flick, Jamie forwarded the mind-blocker code to Alex. One problem at a time. :Hello-Alex. Make this work for me, please.:

:With simulated pleasure, Jamie.:

Right. Now back to the scanner data. What had it picked up here? Jamie parsed the wall with narrowed eyes, the contact lenses doing a digital sweep as she did a visual one.

Definitely an unusual number of bugs, blockers and microcams. They were dealt with easily enough: a quick series of taps on her watch sent a beam out to interfere with them all, setting them on a loop consisting of randomly selected snippets of footage from the last several hours.

It wasn't perfect—someone watching closely would catch the seams between snips—but it would obscure her presence to a casual observer. And there were still over five hours to go until the designated drop time.

Jamie shivered as, a bare instant later, Alex settled a new mini-app into her belt.

:Mind-blocker installed,: Alex's soothing tones announced through her internal comm.

:Thanks.: *Hope it works.*

Huh, was that a buzzball set partway up the wall, buried in the ivy?

No one would plant one of those unless they wanted the ability to keep people out of...

Ha. Jamie allowed herself a quick grin. Obscured by leaves and a clever paint job, below the buzzball was a narrow door. Jamie held her watch against the lockpad and waited for four long seconds while the lockpick mini ran.

A quiet 'snick', barely audible above the crowd's murmurings, announced the unlocking of the door. Jamie let herself in quickly; she might be mostly invisible to digital eyes right now, but a physical observer would still spot a person of approximately her height and build entering the doorway.

It was a fairly standard meeting room, the taste of station cleaner astringent on her tongue, beige walls bare, no furniture save a single, two-person laminex table and accompanying extruded-plastic chairs, all beige, just like the walls. Room for maybe ten people comfortably, twenty if they packed in like it was an elevator. Minicams in the four corners of the room—quickly, if temporarily, dealt with using the counterblock beam.

:Nat, can you check the camera system for feeds… MQWR106, 7, 8 and 9?: she sent, zooming in with her lenses to check the serial codes on the minicams.

A thumbs up flashed in her peripheral vision, the reply message from Nathaniel.

While she waited, Jamie prepped the adhesive on her own minicams, aimed, and threw them up to land right by each of the room's original cameras.

:Got them,: Nathaniel sent.

:Codes for my cams. Switch over plz?:

Jamie stared at her watch intently, waiting for the green flash that would indicate that her own cameras had been spliced into the system, sending footage data back to Aphelion's base security and sending a duplicate stream back to Alex.

The watch flashed green.

Jamie allowed herself a quick smile and sent another message to Nathaniel. :Splice the footage to a loop for me?:

:Already done: was the quick reply. :Backtracked 30m. Feeding them a 28 min loop.:

:You're a gem,: Jamie sent back.

:I know.: A wink emoticon followed, bobbing up at down below eye level in the corner of her left eye until she blinked forcefully to dismiss it.

Jamie threw four buzzballs in the seam of the room's corner, the one at the front away from the door, a foot apart up the wall; if she activated them all at once they'd form an electrical barrier around whatever was in the corner at the time— enemy, her target, whatever. It was bound to come in handy.

She was still trying to think loosely, give herself plenty of options so that she didn't have to commit to a plan that the precog Witch might see.

:Why Witches?: she sent to Nathaniel, partly on a whim. (Partly, though, because of the twist in her gut whenever she thought of the item she was going to retrieve.)

:IDK. I guess that depends on what your target is.:

She let that hang while she set a trap around the table, marking out a circle of conductivity on the floor a couple of paces wide. She tacked the tiny, ball-bearing-sized circuit switch to the floor by the leg of one of the chairs.

She stood, stretching out the small of her back. :When did the last surrofish die out?:

:...???!?!?!!!!:

Jamie sniffed and gave her head a quick shake. Another little trap in the back corner would do nicely. :I'm not here for a surrofish,: she sent. And bit her lip.

Technically, this conversation was already on the edge of illegal. Technically, she'd probably already breached confidence enough that IGP could sack her if they felt like they wanted to.

But...

:What lays gelatinous vacuum eggs up to two feet in diameter?:

:There's a species of turtle that lives in the vacuum out past Incendia. Iridescent, gelatinous eggs.:

A picture of them followed.

Jamie blinked it away. Similar, but not quite the same as what she'd been sent for.

:Pic of surrofish eggs?:

:You are not here to retrieve an SF egg. Tell me you are not.:

:I'm not. They died out what 400 yrs ago.:

A pic flashed up. :Surrofish egg. Last known sighting 2652:

Suck. That one looked exactly like the briefing picture.

But 2652, that was 413 years ago. There was no way surrofish had just randomly appeared again, and no way that the Witches would do anything short of out-and-out warfare if it meant obtaining some again.

Ridiculous. It couldn't be a surrofish, and she was being stupid. MishCon would've warned her if it was something like that.

Jamie ran the pattern scanner over the room, just to check. There. Looked like everything was in place, and she still had—she checked the time—just under five hours now. Plenty of time to get back to security, hunt down the Witches, and stalk them for a bit while she brainstormed, rather than planned.

The door opened.

Time slowed.

It was a black sleeve, the Aphelion Station Security uniform.

Probably coming to do a surveillance check of their own. She could fight her way out and land on the watch list...

He was talking to someone. Jamie froze as she recognised the sound of Adan's voice from the recordings in the briefing packet.

:Hello-Alex?:

:Hello, Jamie.:

:You know that chameleon mini you were working on for me?:

:Yes, I know this mini.:

:How ready is it for field testing?:

:I must advise caution. Your heart rate is elevated, indicating a high-stakes situation, and the data does not show—:

:Hello-Alex! Install chameleon mini *now*!:

A heart-stopping pause, during which the door finished opening, revealing a black-clad, overly conspicuous private security guard—not Aphelion after all, though the uniform was superficially similar—with fair skin and a dark buzz cut.

:Chameleon mini installed.:

The guard stared at the corner where Jamie stood. Blinked. Narrowed his eyes—then relaxed and stepped aside for the Witches to enter, followed by Adan and another guard in black.

Jamie glanced down at herself. Phew. Her entire body—skin, clothing, all of it—had faded to the same nondescript beige as the wall. She could still attract attention to herself through movement or sound—or smell, she supposed—but so long as she stood still and quiet, she'd be okay. For now. Until she thought too loudly about what she was going to do and the precog Witch keyed in on it.

Urgh. And also suck. The Witches were *here*.

But that made sense, she'd sweep the area too if she was getting ready to…

Her heart lurched.

To do a drop.

An unfamiliar trio of people waited at the doorway, eyes hard, jaws set. They were aiming for mean and confident—but Jamie could see the fear in the way their eyes darted from person to person in the room, always circling back to the two Witches, who now stood together to one side of the table. And they had a bag with them, a big black duffle bag on wheels, touristy, brand new—and bulging in a very suspiciously globe-shaped manner.

Jamie inhaled deeply but slowly, silently, and felt the adrenaline flow through her system. Looked like it was show time.

And the only way this show wasn't going to end in disaster for her was to be as erratic… Jamie tilted her head a bare fraction of an inch.

The precog hadn't spotted her.

The precog hadn't spotted her because *they* had been erratic, moving their drop up by five hours, in what Jamie had to admit was a smart move.

But they hadn't figured on her.

Her lips curved into a smile almost as dangerous as her belt.

The drop party were inside, now, door closing behind them. The bag with the egg was still near the threshold. One solid kick would spin it into Jamie's little zone of protection in the corner.

The witches were in the opposite back corner to Jamie. Two securities guards stood in front of them, the third—Security Guard #1, who'd opened the door—between Jamie and the exit.

:Hello-Alex?:

:Hello, Jamie.:

:Engage Sonic Protocol 1.:

:Sonic Protocol 1 engaged.:

Jamie leapt.

The chameleon mini seemed to confuse the guard; he missed the split instant he had to fire.

Jamie wrenched the gun from him.

Backed up an elbow to his face. Cracked him on the back of the skull with the butt of the gun.

One solid kick in the direction of the door sent the duffle bag spinning from its owner's hands. Jamie redirected the spin into the corner, activated the buzzballs.

Blue, sparking electricity flashed in a protective field around it.

Jamie straightened. Eyed the room.

The egg traders had barely moved. Only one had his weapon out.

Or maybe no one else actually *had* weapons, Jamie realised. They'd had to work around Aphelion's rules, just the same as she had.

She grinned. "Thanks for coming to this little meeting," she said. "It's been a *blast*."

She stepped forward next to a chair as the energy field around the table snapped up. The trap in the back corner—Sonic Protocol 1—fired.

A deep, booming sonic wave spread through the chamber.

In this small space, at that low frequency, the effect was immediate: the unshielded occupants dropped writhing to the floor.

In a split instant, the echoes of the wave cut short, absorbed by the shield Alex had erected around the room for that purpose.

Security Guard #1 was down for the count. So was Adan, and one of the egg traders, the one who'd wheeled the bag in.

Like the remaining humans, the male Witch, Rob, sprawled on the floor clutching at his ears, blood trickling through his fingers and from his nose.

The female lay on the floor, knocked unconscious. Looked like she'd hit her head on a chair on the way down. Her left arm lay outflung, her hand and part of her wrist encroaching on Jamie's safe space around the table—which also would have served to keep people in, if that's what she'd ended up needing.

Jamie paced over and kicked the arm out, wrinkling her nose at the stench of burning flesh: the field had severed the arm to the bone. Another half minute and it'd have cut clean through. "Predict that, Witch-bitch."

Witch Rob narrowed his eyes at her, suddenly focused.

A wave of nausea washed over her. The energy field might keep people and sound out, but it wouldn't do anything against the Cerulean Witch's mind-control powers.

Jamie fell to her knees, nausea heaving in her stomach.

Her stomach heaved back, depositing the curry from her last meal aboard Alex on the beige floor. Her mouth and throat burned and she coughed. Spat the acid taste from her mouth, wiped her mouth on her sleeve.

Glanced up at the Cerulean Witch.

He was staring at her, open-mouthed.

Jamie did a quick check of her mental faculties. There was no way really to be sure, but it felt like she was still in control.

The look of wide-eyed disbelief on his face corroborated that.

Apparently, the mind-blocker mini worked.

Shakily, Jamie hauled herself back to her feet. He couldn't hear her through the shield, so she didn't waste effort trying. Instead, she spat again, straightened, and bared her teeth at him.

He scooted backward—right into the back corner that Jamie had accessorised. The sonic wave wasn't the only surprise she'd left there.

Jamie bent down and pressed the circuit switch on the energy shield. The shield fell.

A quick click on her belt. Another buzzball sprang to life.

Witch Rob yelped as the electrical field caught his feet, drawing in on himself, a hunched ball barely contained by the sizzling, sparking blue field.

A third click—but this one wasn't Jamie.

She whirled around toward the sound of a projectile weapon's safety being lifted. Slammed her leg out at the egg trader aiming at her.

Her foot connected with his weapon and it skittered to the floor. It spun across the slick surface, stopping only as it flew into the corner of protection where the bag was. It had enough force to slide partway through the buzzball's field—but the half of it that made it through was melted slag.

She pivoted to the remaining security guard. Before she'd taken a step in his direction, he sidestepped to the table, stooped to the floor— and the energy shield snapped up around him.

Jamie nodded. Plausible deniability. He wouldn't hurt her, and it would look like that hadn't been his choice.

She could live with that.

She whirled to the protected corner and tapped out a quick sequence on her watch to deactivate the buzzballs. The black duffle bag smelled of propane gas, same as a lot of old-style hot water systems did, with a hint of something sweet and berry-ish—and it was heavier than it looked. She was loving the wheels right about now.

:Nat priority escort NOW.:

She sent a second message through to Alex. :Hello-Alex, begin launch sequence five-three-oh-seven-delta immediately.:

:Launch sequence activated.:

:Yo how hot:

She glanced around the room as she pulled the bag to heel beside her.

A whimper drew her attention in the corner by the door.

Acid-sucking... Now that was not good form, forgetting one of the players.

Jamie squinted. Looked like she wasn't the only one with an operational chameleon mini. Guy was nearly indistinguishable from the beige wall.

She raised a hand. "I'm with IGP," she said, though it wasn't often a thing she admitted to in public. "This egg is under confiscation orders."

The man—difficult to say what he looked like with the chameleon mini running—nodded. "Take... Take it," he said hoarsely. "But..." He did something that was probably licking his lips. "Don't let IGP have it."

Jamie blinked. "What?"

"Surro..."

Jamie went cold.

"Surrofish egg. Destroy it."

Her grip tightened on the bag. She strode from the room. Locked it behind her. And walked on out of Sector Q as though she didn't have the means for the destruction of humanity tucked away in a flimsy black bag.

"Now what?" Nathaniel perched on the silver edge of the control desk, in front of one of the big screens currently completing the exit sequence as they glided away from Aphelion. His fire-coloured hair glowed oddly in the blue light, and his eyes gleamed.

Jamie would have liked to believe it was only the blue tint of the light that was turning his expression sickly, but she'd known him long enough that she recognised in his face the same knot of horror she felt herself.

"I don't know." She sat at the desk in her moulded pilot's chair.

The room was crowded with Nathaniel here. She could feel his body heat.

Alex—as in the entire shuttle—shook.

"The hell?" Nathaniel gripped the desk with pale-knuckled hands.

Pulse racing, Jamie jabbed frantically at the control panel. "Hello-Alex, get me data, stat. What the hell is happening?"

But Alex didn't need to reply, because a giant face took over Jamie's screen, and there, frowning down at her, was Mitch Bonavich, her blond-haired, dark-eyed, clean-shaven handler at the IGP.

The gleam in his eyes didn't do wonders for the speed of her pulse.

"Bonavich." Jamie nodded cautiously. "Why are you rattling my ship?"

Nathaniel pressed himself to the side wall, trying to keep out of view. Sensible.

Surrofish egg.

Don't let the IGP have it.

Bonavich smiled nastily. "I have a problem with your current trajectory."

The IGP having the surrofish egg would be a damn sight better than letting the Witches get it... But nothing in Jamie's relatively long (considering her age) history with the IGP had actually done much to reassure her that they'd be any more responsible with how they deployed the egg.

Witches were Witches, and Jamie wasn't going to cry herself to sleep at night if they all suddenly vanished from the universe... But on the other hand, she'd heard that there were cures now, that some of them could be cleaned, could be saved...

And when it came down to it, weren't most wars fought because the upper crust wanted more money or power or territory, and not because the general populations actually had anything against each other?

Probably, there were Witches out there like her, just as much a slave to their system as she was to hers.

She smiled back at the screen, letting some of her delighted defiance creep into her eyes.

IGP could go stick themselves.

"You have a problem with my trajectory, do you? Well I have a problem with you interfering with my shuttle."

Bonavich narrowed his eyes. "Your orders were to bring the item directly to Headquarters, Ms Evans. I assume you have not forgotten the way?"

Nathaniel was not-breathing so concertedly, Jamie could feel his tension from here.

"Space is big," Jamie said prettily. "I didn't realise there was only one way to get to HQ."

This time, Bonavich's smile didn't touch his eyes.

Alex shook again, the whole shuttle jolting unpleasantly.

Maintaining eye contact with Bonavich, Jamie tapped out a sequence on the secondary keyboard that sat below the main level of the desks, out of view of the screens. A quick thought, and she relayed an accompanying message to Nat as well. :Brace.:

"Ms Evans, let me make myself clear. You hold an incredibly da—*precious* cargo right now, and if you do not bring it immediately to HQ for surrender, we will be forced to take control of your ship."

Jamie could feel the tension in her own smile, not because she was concerned by Bonavich's threats, but because trying to activate Alex's defensive system while programming an escape sequence while plotting a course for the nearest bit of space IGP wouldn't enter while also trying to keep track of the conversation was taxing her brain power.

A little.

A fraction.

Just a tiny bit.

:Three,: she sent to Nathaniel.

In her peripheral vision, he slid silently to the ground and sprawled out on his back, feet and legs tucked under the desk, head sticking out into the corridor beyond the small room, arms bracing against the door frame.

Sensible. It was about to get bouncy in here, and at least flat on the floor his body would spread out the impact somewhat.

"Sure," Jamie said, beaming up a more convincing smile at Bonavich. "I'll be right over."

:Two.:

Bonavich's dark eyes narrowed again. "Ms Evans, if you—"

Jamie didn't wait for him to finish. :One.: "Hello-Alex, sequence seven-nine-six-three-oh.

See ya!" She flashed Bonavich a final grin then thumped a button to kill the transmission.

Alex shuddered, then jolted like an electrified eel.

The seat harness cut into Jamie's shoulders.

On the floor, Nathaniel cried out, his head narrowly missing the door frame.

A straining creak.

Alarm systems burst into chorus, wild beeps and klaxons.

"Gravity waves incoming." Alex's calm voice sounded ridiculous against the backdrop of screaming metal and thumps.

Jamie laced her hands behind her neck, curled her head forward to protect her spine. "Brace!" she screamed at Nathaniel.

Acid-sucking contagion, he was going to die. He was going to die here like this, flung around the control room like a ragdoll, and it was her fault.

The straining rose in pitch to become a whine, the metal hull protesting as the IGP's gravity waves tried to force them in one direction, while Alex tried to follow the counter sequence Jamie had plotted and force the shuttle in the opposite direction. For one heart-stopping moment, Jamie thought the IGP might win.

Then, with one more heart-rattling shudder and a roar of metal like thunder, Alex tore free of the IGP's grip and bulleted away.

We made it.

Jamie sagged against her harness, head pounding. :Nat?:

Her head hurt, her shoulders hurt, and now that she thought about it, her left pinky hurt too. Might have snapped it, bashing it against the desk.

Groggily, she forced her head around.

Nat lay sprawled on the floor, eyes closed, left side of his face already purpling with an impressive bruise. :Nat!:

:Dont talk:

Jamie exhaled. *Thank you,* she muttered to whomever might be listening. *Thank you.*

:Next time,: Nat sent, :just leave me on the station.:

"You've been nagging me for *years* to come with," Jamie said, one side of her mouth lifting in a tired smirk. "One little taste of freedom and you want to go running back to Aphelion? Ha. Softie."

:When I can stand up again ur going t b ver sorry.:

"When—" Jamie swallowed. :When you can stand up again, I'm going to be very, very relieved.:

:Is it always like this?:

Jamie glanced over the screens, the course she'd plotted for the farther most reaches of inhabited space now visible, flickering up and down as Alex added calculations around it to improve their speed and fuel efficiency, to plan refuelling stops—and to keep them in hyper-space as much as possible, so the IGP couldn't track them.

"No," Jamie said. "It's very much not usually like this."

But then again, it wasn't her first time on the run from someone either, so maybe it was.

Either way, at least this time she'd have com-pany.

Far distant, at the outer reaches of inhabited space, Alex came slowly to a stop. A gentle 'ding' echoed through the ship, and Alex's soothing, even voice sounded. "You have arrived at your destination."

In the tiny scullery, Jamie snorted. "Hilarious, Alex." She set down the bar of chocolate the transmatter had just finished constructing for her, licked her fingers for the sweet, sugary hit, and headed to the control room.

Nathaniel met her there. His flame-orange hair was too long to spike effectively these days, but the length had revealed a propensity to curl in ways that Jamie had told him were spectacularly more adorable than the spikes anyway.

He raised his eyebrows in greeting, and Jamie slipped into the control room, pulse oddly tangible in her chest.

She drew in a slow breath as she surveyed the data glowing blue on the large, transparent screens.

A slow exhale. "We're here."

Obviously, Alex wouldn't have told them they'd arrived for nothing, but still. Nearly nine months they'd been on the run from the IGP, hopping in and out of normal-space to let Alex's warp drive reboot, and otherwise spending all their time in hyperspace, sliding between the waves of physical reality like a dolphin skimming through the sea as they leap-frogged their way to the outermost reaches of the galaxy.

Nathaniel grabbed Jamie's hand as she returned to the corridor, heading toward the secondary airlock where the egg had been stashed.

Jamie squeezed Nathaniel's proffered hand and shot him a grateful look.

"We're doing the right thing, right?" he said. They peered through the window of the airlock, the giant pearl of an egg—squishy and semi-opaque—sitting in front of them, the dark reaches of space beyond visible through the airlock's outer windows. Few stars sparkled this far from the centre of the galaxy.

Still probably not far enough.

"Of course." Jamie shot him a tight smile. "IGP would have started a war with it."

Nathaniel pursed his lips. "Not sure we won't end up with one of those regardless."

Not least because of the one thing they'd both stopped saying since early on in their journey: What if this wasn't the last egg? What if the IGP had others?

But Jamie hit the red button to vacuum seal the airlock door anyway. It closed away the lingering propane-and-berry scent of the egg, and the dry, cool air of Alex's recycling system washed over her.

IGP's data in that initial briefing Jamie had received so long ago had been good: the egg was essentially indestructible, impervious to fire, water, pressure and vacuum alike. It resisted physical harm, resealing any openings made in its surface within moments.

In the end, Jamie had respected its sheer determination to live, and had decided she didn't actually want to kill it anyway.

So here they were. Months away at best from human-occupied space, and Witch Clan Space was further beyond that again.

They'd calculated the trajectories. Assuming it didn't hatch earlier, the egg should end up crossing paths with a habitable neighbouring galaxy in about two hundred thousand standard years' time. Implausibly long for any planet-bound life, but the creatures who lived out in the black were cryo-adapted to long, accidental journeys between viable habitats.

Jamie could only hope it ended up somewhere it would be allowed to live, without its life being co-opted or interfered with.

She clung to Nathaniel's hand. "Hello-Alex?"

"Hello, Jamie."

"Space it."

The outer doors slid open.

The egg sailed out into the black.
A life without interference sounded amazing.

ABOUT THE AUTHOR

AMY LAURENS is an award-winning Australian author of fantasy and science fiction for both adults and young adults.

She has written the award-winning portal-fantasy *Sanctuary* series about Edge, a 13-year-old girl forced to move to a small country town because of witness protection (the first book is *Where Shadows Rise*), the humorous fantasy *Kaditeos* series, following newly-graduated Evil Overlord Mercury as she attempts to acquire a castle, the young adult *Storm Foxes* series about love and magic and mental health, and a whole host of non-fiction, usually about dogs and writing.

You can find out more at www.amylaurens.com.

WITH THANKS TO…

Liana Brooks (as ever), Dean Wesley Smith, my fantabulous husband, the amazing fans who backed this project on Kickstarter, and God. This book would have been less without you <3

HOW NOT TO ACQUIRE A CASTLE

On a hard plastic chair in the front row of the Great Hall in the world's fifth-best Evil Overlording Academy, with its red-wooden parquetry floor that spoke of wealth and the beige, square panels of soundboards speaking of conservatism on the walls, Mercury sat, pointedly not sweating.

Partly, this was because the Academy Administrators had deigned to turn on the air-conditioning earlier in the day, in recognition of the fact that the hall would be packed out with approximately six hundred bodies, all here to celebrate the graduation of about a third of that crowd.

But mostly, Mercury was pointedly not sweating because she made it a point never to sweat, sweat being an indication that she was working hard, and hard work being antithetical to her way of life.

However. If she *had* been sweating right now, it would not have been due to the uncomfortable warmth of six hundred packed bodies that even the air-conditioning system couldn't completely shift, or, in fact, from over-exertion. Instead, it would have been caused by an even more unfamiliar concept in Mercury's emotional vocabulary: nervousness.

Mercury did not *get* nervous. Mercury got things *done*.

So the fact that she was sitting here, in the front row of the Great Hall, about to graduate from Evil Overlording Academy (with distinction), and was feeling *nervous*... She crumpled the black paper program in her pale fists. It made her furious, that's what it did. Abjectly furious, that snooty-tooty Deviran with his stupid morals and his stupid I-don't-want-to-be-here and his stupid Overlords-are-empty-figureheads and his stupid face sitting ten people over, looking implacable with his deep brown skin and barely-there, precision-groomed beard, as though he knew it gave him a stupid air of alluringly stupid mystery...

Mercury scowled and searched for the train of thought that had been derailed, yet again, by Deviran's stupidity.

Ah. Yes. She was angry because she was nervous because she wasn't absolutely entirely one hundred and fifty percent sure that she'd beaten Deviran in their final exams, and 1) being anything less than a hundred and fifty percent certain of anything made her cranky, and 2) being beaten by Deviran for dux of the year would be utterly unbearable. She flicked away a piece of fluff that had become snagged under her immaculately magenta-painted nails and smoothed out the black paper program.

In the front corner of the hall, the starkly-attired string quartet with their traditional black instruments began playing the March of the Oncoming Doom. The screechy scrapes of hundreds of chairs on the hall's wooden floor sounded as the crowd climbed to its collective feet.

Mercury sat with her arms firmly folded for a few moments longer, until her best friend Sparky kicked her in the ankle.

"Get up, idiot," Sparky hissed, hints of real flame flickering through her flame-coloured pixie cut.

"No," Mercury said, flouncing to her feet and tossing her own glossy brown hair back over her shoulders. Four years she'd been playing by the Academy's rules in order to get what she wanted, and she'd had just about enough. Other people's rules should only be applied to plebs too stupid to invent their own.

Sparky rolled her eyes somewhere over Mercury's head before focusing on the stage, where the ceremonial party had begun entering.

Mercury clenched her jaw and narrowed her own eyes as the teachers of the Evil Overlording Academy filed onto the stage, dressed in their formal finery. Each teacher had their own distinctive look that matched their personality and their Overlording style, from severe charcoal suits to jet-black leathers, pastel ballgowns and gem-toned lingerie and eye-blinding spandex, and even on one tiny old woman at the back, worn jeans and a grey flannel shirt. She was the one to watch out for, of course; Mercury could respect an Overlord who was confident enough in their abilities that they didn't need to telegraph them. It wasn't a look *she* would consider, of course, but still. She could respect it.

The band's march finished and, after a moderately awkward pause, the crowd sat. The Principal, pale skin and dark hair matching his suspiciously vampiric red-and-black suit, took the podium, and Mercury narrowed her eyes. He was doing a superb job of hiding his emotions—he was a premier Evil Overlord, after all—but she was Mercury, and unlike anyone else, she had the benefit of being able to rummage through people's consciousnesses. She was better at adding things *into* people's minds than taking information out, but he was telegraphing fear loudly enough that she could sense it without trying overly much.

Mercury pursed her lips. Hmm.

The Principal cleared his throat at the blackened-wood podium, and the fear made it into his usually-unreadable eyes. "Before we begin," he said, and Mercury's stomach did a peculiar kind of flip-flop. "I have a pressing announcement to make regarding the safety of our students and their families."

He cleared his throat again and took out a sheet of paper from his pocket, unfolding it carefully and smoothing out the creases before beginning again. "The Council"—quiet booing echoed around the hall, and Mercury tsked impatiently—"have asked me to recommend that students from Tumul Tuos seriously consider postponing their return to town for a few days. The city is dealing with a *situation* at present which may present a danger to our students' health and safety."

Mercury's hands fisted at her sides and she forced herself to remain seated. What was wrong with her city? What had the Council mucked up now? A risk to the students' safety?

There had to be more he wasn't telling them. Gently, Mercury tugged on his consciousness, implanting the suggestion that it might be better to share the news than to keep it secret. After all, how could they fight an enemy they didn't know?

"There are, ah…" He trailed off, glancing side to side as though wondering why his mouth had decided to continue.

Mercury didn't snicker, but she did press her lips together in satisfaction.

The Principal took a deep, steadying breath and seemed to change tack. "There has been one death already. The family have already been notified, so it is with much regret that I must inform you that Woovermyer will no longer be with us at the Evil Overlording Academy."

Murmurs broke out around the room, not all of them sad—to be expected in a school devoted to raising the next generation of dictators (ish) and despots (of sorts).

Mercury, however, crushed her program in her left hand, fist so tight her nails bit her palm.

"You okay?" Sparky murmured, leaning toward her.

Mercury gave a single, tense shake of her head and stared at the podium. Dead. Livie Woovermyer was dead in *her city*. And the Council hadn't done anything to stop it. Couldn't do anything to stop it, probably, given they'd warned the students to stay away. Livie hadn't been the strongest candidate in the year level, but she was no lightweight, either. It would take a lot of power to kill a Seven.

Enough was enough.

A good thing Mercury was about to graduate

at the top of the class, giving her the right to knock the lowest ranking current Overlord off their perch. Tumul Tuos would be hers in a matter of hours. And then there'd be no more of these wasteful deaths. Her city would be safe at last.

Madame Pompadour was up the front now, elbow gloves the same glimmery silver colour as her elaborate, piled-curls wig, eyelids gleaming with matching silver eye shadow, and abruptly Mercury realised Madame was there to make the announcement that would change her life forever.

She leaned forward in her seat, ready to stand when her name was called.

"And now the announcement you've all been dying for," the Political Alliances teacher trilled, the frills on her evening gown fluttering as she moved. "The dux of this year's cohort!"

Sweat slicked Mercury's palms. Irritated, she reached over and wiped them on Sparky's thigh.

Sparky pushed Mercury's hands back into her own personal space bubble and Mercury, nervous to the edge of distraction, let her.

"Will you please join me in welcoming to the stage, our wonderful dux for this year, Deviran Goodsmith!"

Mercury froze halfway to standing. "Did she just say Deviran?" she whispered furiously to Sparky.

Sparky hauled her forcibly back down into her seat. "Yes," she hissed back. "Sit down, you're making a fool of yourself."

Mercury's spine snapped upright as she sat, and she arranged the folds of her long black skirt demurely. "No I'm not." She closed her eyes. "Deviran's going up to the stage, isn't he?" Even at a whisper, the misery in her voice was clear, but this time, she didn't care.

Sparky reached over and squeezed her hand.

Mercury squeezed back, lacing her fingers back through Sparky's, and held tight as all her plans and dreams vanished in front of her.

A stone had landed in her chest. That must be it. Some strange sort of magic that made her chest contract and sink, and made the world distort for just a moment, long enough to trick her into thinking Deviran had beaten her so that someone could jump in front of her and yell SURPRISE!

Any moment now.

Any moment.

She refused to open her eyes and watch Deviran parading across the stupid stage like some stupid stupid-person, receiving his stupid medal and stupid symbolic crest pin.

It was that last exam question. She'd known Deviran would pull out his ridiculous 'Evil Overlords are merely figureheads, the Business Guild is where the power really lies' rant that everyone had heard a million times back when he was younger and angrier, and she'd tried to counter it, she really had.

She'd argued for the importance of the Overlording position, for the power of having a symbolic figure to unite the population in their hatred, for having a person able to make all the difficult, necessary decisions the Council was too weak and spineless to make... But it hadn't been enough. Everything she'd worked for, everything she'd set out to prove—and it wasn't enough.

There were words, there were names, and then forever later, once she'd died twice already, Sparky elbowed her in the ribs. "Come on," Sparky muttered. "We're up next."

And sure enough, there was a shuffling of presenters as the last of the Powers Behind The Throne graduates departed the stage, and the next speaker announced in threatening, funereal tones, "The Overlording cohort."

Mercury blinked furiously and followed Sparky to the end of the line at the right side of the stage. The other candidates proceeded one at a time across the stage, two girls and then stupid Deviran, and then a handful more and then Sparky, and then the speaker was calling her name.

Hands fisted, Mercury tossed her head high, climbed the four steps, and marched across the stage. She wouldn't look at them, the stupid faculty who'd denied her the city she rightfully deserved, and she wouldn't look the other way either, at the classmates and crowd undoubtedly sniggering at her failure.

She shook hands with the presenter, and while he pinned the tiny crossed-swords badge on her collar, her eyes betrayed her and slid toward the audience. Her stomach flipped as she saw the crowd of parents and friends behind the rows of students, all the way to the back of the hall, twenty rows at least, illuminated by the late afternoon light streaming in through the ceiling-high windows to the right. Everyone had someone here to watch them graduate. Everyone except Weird Al—and her.

The presenter finished with her pin, muttered something to her, and offered his hand again.

Mercury coldly ignored it and strode from the stage. It didn't matter. None of it mattered. Tumul Tuos was her city anyway, and no one could change that. She'd think of something. She'd take a day or two out, make some plans...

And she could always hope that Deviran would choose some other Overlording territory. He'd be stupid to, but then again, he was stupid, so. Mercury could hope.

All at once, mid-way down the steps off the stage, Mercury came to rigid attention, scanning the room.

Somewhere out there in the crowd, an exchange of power had just taken place, and it felt... unusual.

But the final few students were backing up behind her and muttering, so Mercury headed back toward her seat, craning her head all the while and searching for some sign of whatever it was that had just discharged a dizzyingly quiet amount of power into the room.

She sat, and Sparky leaned over. "Okay?"

"Mm," said Mercury. "Did you feel..." She accidentally caught the eye of the student behind her and twisted back to face the front.

"Feel what?"

Mercury turned it over in her mind. It had felt

like a large shot of power discharged very quietly—but perhaps it hadn't been. Perhaps it had only been a small discharge after all, something most people wouldn't have noticed.

But still, something about it had tugged on her. It very nearly felt like something she'd felt before, only she *knew* she'd never sensed that kind of discharge. She shook her head. "Never mind. Don't worry."

Sparky sighed and straightened. "It's fine, Mercury," she said, drily exasperated. "I know you didn't win, but I promise, you'll live through it."

Mercury waved a hand for silence.

The power had just discharged again, and it had come from somewhere in the back corner, far away from the windows and light.

Impatiently, Mercury waited for the formalities to conclude. The crowd stood while the quartet played the exit march, and the stage party left, Mercury tapping her foot all the while.

The moment the last notes of the march died away, Mercury turned and headed to the back corner, weaving in and out of the students and parents who had seemed to explode slowly but inexorably out from the neat rows of seating, ignoring Sparky's calls behind her. Power, something that tugged in a way that was strange and familiar, all at once. She pushed her way through a family posing for pictures—and halted.

In the shadows of the back corner, Deviran stood with his family, with his stupid, smug little smile, looking as tall and dark and stupidly alluring as ever. Prat.

His mother, short but sleek, and his father— tall, and utterly terrifying in a way not at all diminished by his gleaming smile—gushed over him, patting his back and hugging him tight. Within moments the Principal was there, glibly shaking hands and congratulating them on the success of their son. Something flickered across his consciousness, and also Deviran's father's— some moment of recognition in response to what they were saying. But Mercury brushed it aside just as the mother brushed melodramatic tears from her cheeks and handed Deviran a silver-wrapped package about as long as her hand but half the width.

That. That was the source of the strange, magical feeling. Mercury watched hawk-eyed as Deviran unwrapped the gift. A glimpse of gold set her pulse racing—What was it? What did it do? Could she steal it?—and then the paper fell away to the floor, and Deviran stood staring wordlessly at the object in his hands, and Mercury did too.

Wide-eyed, Deviran raised his gaze to his parents, and even from where she stood Mercury could hear the reverence in his voice as he thanked them.

But Mercury had eyes only for the object. No wonder she'd felt it discharge, and no wonder it had felt both strange and familiar. In Deviran's hands lay a glorious, sunshine-gold key, large and strong—and with a handle in the shape of a stylised fish, long, flowing fins curving to make the grip.

A Key. They'd given him a Key. And not just any Key, but *the* Key, *her* Key, the Artefact of Power belonging to *her* city.

A wordless noise of wanting rose in Mercury's throat. Who cared about being dux? She needed that Key.

Keep reading! Head to
www.amylaurens.com/books/
kaditeos/castle/
to buy your copy now!